WITHDRAWN FROM

The Battle Disk of Troy

Written by Alison Leonard
Illustrated by Damon Burnard

Other stories in the
Computer Whizzkids
series:

The Magnificent Dream Disk

The Write-It-Right Computer

Marybelle and her Computer Aunt

C707355299

For Adèle Geras

ORCHARD BOOKS
96 Leonard Street, London EC2A 4RH
Orchard Books Australia
14 Mars Road, Lane Cove, NSW 2066

First published in Great Britain in 1996
Text copyright © Alison Leonard, 1996
Illustrations copyright © Damon Burnard 1996
ISBN 1 85213 794 0

The right of Alison Leonard to be identified as the author
and Damon Burnard to be identified as the illustrator of
this work has been asserted by them in accordance with the
Copyright, Designs and Patents Act, 1988
A CIP catalogue for this book is available from the British
Library
Printed in Great Britain

Contents

Chapter One

Carolyn stared out of the window down into the back yard. Behind her, Matt was grunting away as he pounded the joy-pad on the computer.

"Wow – I've spiked fifteen Trojans! – Ugh, they've crushed me and twenty other Greeks!" It was their new computer game, *Trojan War*.

Carolyn and Matt were twins. They used to be best friends as well. But, since they'd got the computer, they'd fought. Fought like cat and dog, fought like Greek and Trojan, fought like . . . well, like brother and sister.

Down in the back yard stood a horse. Not a real horse – the twins' back yard was too tiny to fit a horse that needed space to gallop. This was a hollow wooden horse, big as a caravan, and their dad was hammering the last few nails into a trapdoor in its body.

Matt refused to look at it. "It's stupid, building a flipping great horse like that, just for a school play."

Carolyn explained to him over and over again. "It's the Trojan horse, dumbo! It's supposed to win the Trojan war for the Greeks!"

"Stop yacking," said Matt. "You're ruining my concentration." Grunt.

Carolyn's stop-watch went *Ping*! "My turn!" she cried, and rushed over to the computer. As usual, Matt refused to budge, and then they started fighting again . . .

In the beginning, Dad told them the story. The real story, the original story.

How beautiful Helen, in long ago Greece, was married to a Greek king. But the handsome Prince of Troy, called Paris, came and won her heart and Helen sailed away with him. Her Greek husband sailed after her with a thousand ships, and the Trojan War began.

Ten years later, the war of Greek against Trojan for the beautiful Helen was still raging – until the Greeks found a cunning weapon that would carry them into the heart of the besieged city of Troy . . .

And Dad told them what happened in the end. But Carolyn refused to believe it.

"She's so beautiful . . ." breathed Carolyn. Her ears were shut, her eyes were fixed on the screen. She'd shoved Matt off the computer seat and grabbed her turn. "Helen," she murmured, "I'll turn the game around for you. I'll win the war for the brave Trojans, not the beastly battling Greeks."

Matt wasn't listening. He was pacing up and down impatiently.

Hammer – hammer – hammer! came from the yard. Dad was a teacher at the High School, and the huge horse was to be the star of the school play about the Trojan War. But the horse wasn't ready – and the dress rehearsal was tomorrow.

Ping! went the stop-watch again. Matt pushed Carolyn off the seat. "You've got the Trojans all lined up, Caro! Why haven't you zapped them? The Greeks have *got* to win, you know!"

"I don't see why," said Carolyn. "Why shouldn't Helen run off with her handsome prince?"

Matt bashed away at the joy-pad. "All my Greek ships are sailing away! They're giving up!" He jerked the ships crazily to and fro.

"Don't be daft," said Carolyn. "They're only pretending, the cunning old Greeks. They'll hide behind the island, like Dad said. Look, that island there. Then they'll sneak back with their great wooden horse . . ."

Matt still didn't listen. He didn't even hear Carolyn declare, "I won't let it happen! I'm going to save Troy, and make Paris and Helen live happily ever after!"

But how? Zapping was all very well. But she needed a secret weapon to match the wooden horse. Not arrows, not swords, not even boiling oil would do.

Dad was calling from downstairs. "Kids! Off the computer now – it's time for bed!"

Late into the night, Carolyn lay wide awake. She couldn't think of anything but the computer game. Dad said the Greeks had *got* to win, because they won in history. But couldn't she change history?

At last she fell asleep – straight into a dream about Helen of Troy.

Helen stood there, larger than life, and ghostly, with long flowing hair and white flowing robes.

Below the image of Helen stood a horse. This horse wasn't wooden. It was real, but dream-like, and it was galloping over an ancient landscape. Its colour was rust, and its mane and tail flew in the wind. The landscape around it was littered with swords and arrows and dead human bodies.

The horse held something in its mouth. In the dream, Carolyn knew that this was the weapon she needed. She held out her hand and begged the horse to give it to her. But the horse galloped past her.

Tears poured from Helen's beautiful eyes. "Help me!" she wept.

The horse must have heard her. It turned and, with a gracious gesture, let its precious gift fall on to Carolyn's hand. Helen smiled through her tears.

Carolyn looked down dreamily. She was holding a computer disk. It wasn't the usual boring blue or black. It was rust-brown, like the horse. In her dream, she saw what was written on it:

The TROJAN DISK

How to change history, and win the war for Troy.

Chapter Two

In the morning Carolyn and Matt set off for school.

Their dad must have been down in the back yard half the night. He'd borrowed a trailer to put the Trojan horse on and take it to the High School. But the horse was too big, and he couldn't get it through the gate.

Anyone could see he needed help. But Dad was proud. He had to do things on his own.

In assembly, they sat at the back as usual, muttering about computer games. Lots of different gangs swapped disks and discussed strategies. They never talked about anything else.

"Silence, children!" ordered the Head. "Stand, and go quietly back to your classrooms!" Carolyn turned to walk out after Matt.

She felt something under her foot. Something flat and hard. She looked down. It was a computer disk.

"Hey!" she said to herself. "What's this?" She bent down and swiftly picked it up.

In the classroom, she glanced at Matt. Had he noticed the disk? No, he was taking out his maths book. No one else had noticed. The disk had fallen in *her* path. It was hers.

She slid it out of her pocket. It was just like the one in her dream! It was rust-brown, with the label: *The Trojan Disk. How to change history, and win the war for Troy.*

After school, Carolyn couldn't wait to get home and put her secret disk in the computer. But it wasn't that easy.

The first problem was, Matt could run quicker than her, and was bound to get there first.

The second problem was, the back gate was blocked by a crowd of Matt's school friends. They were laughing at Dad, who was still hammering. Now he was pulling nails *out* of the horse, not bashing them *into* it. He was taking off its legs, so that he could get it out through the back gate.

"'Scuse us, *please*! This *is* our house, you know!" Matt and Carolyn barged through the crowd.

"You know what?" said Matt gloomily, glaring at the computer. "Dad'll make us go and watch this play of his, up at the High." Then – "Hey, look at this! It says: *You have discovered the secret weapon of the Greeks*! It's a wooden horse!"

While Matt was finding out what to do with the wooden horse in the computer, Carolyn looked out of the window at Dad's real wooden horse. It lay on its side in the yard, legless. The kids hooted with laughter.

"Poor old Dad," said Carolyn. "Go down, Matt. Tell your mates to stop tormenting him."

Miraculously, Matt took one look out of the window, then dashed downstairs.

She was alone. She could try out the mysterious disk. She slipped it into the computer in place of the ordinary one, pressed the joy-pad, and . . .

Carolyn obeyed.

When she opened them again, she saw, prancing across the screen, a beautiful rust-coloured horse. It was the horse she'd seen in last night's dream. Behind its flowing mane, it drew words of instruction:

follow the magic horse. Do not follow the wooden horse. The wooden horse will deceive and destroy...

She moved the joy-pad gently where the dream-horse was leading.

The horse led her out of Troy and up into the hills. Down below lay the sleeping city. Beyond, moonlight sparkled on the sea, and far away, on the horizon, lay the island where the Greek armies were hiding.

In a valley on the steep side of the mountain, Carolyn saw the entrance to a dark cave.

The horse urged her on with its flowing mane : *Come*! *Farther*! *On* – *on*! And it led her into the mouth of the cave.

Slowly her eyes got used to the dark. The cave hummed with murmuring voices. Swords glinted in the light of torches that flickered at the far end. Armour clanked and echoed against the stone walls. Carolyn heard one word murmured over and over again: " Helen! Helen!"

She felt as if she *was* one of those soldiers in their clanking, echoing armour. She stood next to Paris in the flickering light of the cave.

"Are you ready, men?" asked Paris. "Shall we go to fight the Greeks and make Helen mine for ever?"

"Yes! We will!" The words came from the soldiers in a low roar.

Carolyn heard her own voice among them. "We will!"

As they paused at the mouth of the cave, she could see the great stone walls of the city below. But what was that on the sandy shore beyond? The wooden horse – a gift from the cunning Greeks!

She looked round at her fellow soldiers. Their eyes were fixed on the man in front. They'd been fighting for ten long years, and they were weary. She must bring them magic through her precious disk. How?

"Helen!" she breathed. "Helen!"

In a flash, Helen stood in front of them. Her hair gleamed in the moonlight, and her dress was filmy and white. But over it she was wearing armour, and in her hand she carried a gleaming white sword. She was smiling.

No, thought Carolyn: that's not a smile, that's a *grin*.

I'm sick of being useless and beautiful," said Helen. "Come on, Paris. Come down into Troy and fight this last battle – with me at your side!"

Then – *Crash*!

Chapter Three

Carolyn blinked. She was still sitting in front of the computer.

The crash had come from outside – from down in the yard, or the street beyond.

She went over to the window.

Dad and Matt stood staring at the wooden Trojan horse. The yard was scattered with hammers and the rest of Dad's tools. They'd dragged the legless horse out through the yard gate, and it had just crashed over on to its side.

Next morning Dad had a face like thunder as he munched his breakfast.

"What's up, Dad?" asked Matt. He'd forgotten it was the dress rehearsal that night.

"You can't have a Trojan War without a Trojan Horse!" He got up, still munching toast.

"I've promised it'll be ready for the performance tomorrow. They'll just have to *pretend* there's a horse tonight, that's all!" As she watched him stomp off down the road, Carolyn caught sight of a High School girl among the gang of boys who waved at him. There was something familiar about the way she held her tennis racket in her hand – like a shining sword.

After school, Matt worked away on the computer. His Greeks had left the wooden horse on the beach near the gates of Troy, and now they sailed back to the island to get their boats and weapons ready.

"Don't you want a go, Caro?" asked Matt, puzzled.

"No, thanks," said Carolyn, airily. "You can work away all you like. The Trojans will win in the end."

"They won't," said Matt. He went on grunting away at the joy-pad. "It's not history, anyway. It's only a story. What they call a legend – a myth. But you still can't change the ending."

Grunt, grunt, grunt. He was anchoring his ships and putting his Greek sailors in small craft to row back into shore.

All was set for the final battle.

Carolyn lay in bed, eyes wide open. She heard Dad come in and stomp about like an angry Greek. The dress rehearsal had not gone well.

She waited until his bedroom door was firmly shut, then waited still longer. Could she hear him snoring? Yes. She crept out, along the landing, and loaded the rust-brown disk into the computer. She closed her eyes and followed the prancing horse with its flowing mane.

Next, she was in full bronze armour, marching beside Helen down the mountain towards Troy. Helen lifted her shining white sword high in the air, and Carolyn lifted hers alongside.

Helen was muttering. Carolyn leaned closer to hear what she was saying.

"I'm not just a pretty face!" she protested. "I want a share of the action!"

As they drew near the city, Carolyn could hear the chatterings of the Trojans. Some of them had spotted the wooden horse, and she watched them drag it up from the beach to the city gates. They were met by other citizens of Troy and there was a heated argument.

"It's dangerous!"

"No, it's a gift from the gods!"

The greedy side won. "Yes – a gift from the gods! We must take it into the city, and celebrate!"

The gates of Troy creaked open. The horse groaned as the Trojans dragged it through.

Then the gates clanged shut. From the mountainside Carolyn and the rest of Paris's soldiers heard sounds of partying and music from the city as the feasting began.

Paris's troops followed Helen and Carolyn faithfully as they approached Troy. Paris was bringing up the rear. "I thought that was the best place to put him," said Helen, grinning. "He's not all that bright, is he?"

Carolyn was puzzled. Wasn't Helen supposed to be in love with the handsome Paris?

"What are we going to do now?" she asked.

March into the city, of course," replied Helen, "and tell them not to be such fools with that horse. Anyone can see it's got Greek soldiers hiding inside!"

Helen's shining sword opened the massive gates like magic, and closed them like magic behind her. She and Carolyn strode on towards the sound of the party, with Paris's army following.

They were not a moment too soon. The Trojans were drunk. Already they were bowing down to worship the horse as their new god.

"Trojans!" cried Helen. "Stop your celebrations!" The Trojans obeyed instantly. "Now – sleep!" Straight away, they fell into a drunken slumber. "Wake up when you're fit to fight!" Then she turned to Carolyn. "Stand watch over that Greek horse. Make sure no Greek soldier escapes out of the trapdoor."

Carolyn glowed with pride. She stood tall, sword at the ready, and gazed fiercely at the trapdoor in the belly of the wooden horse.

Chapter Four

BANG! - Hammer hammer. CRASH!

What was that noise? Had some Trojans woken up? Were they clashing their weapons to threaten the Greeks?

BANG! Hammer hammer. CRASH!

Carolyn blinked and shook herself. The noise didn't come from Troy. It came from outside the window.

She ran over. Yes – Dad was out on the pavement in the moonlight. He was trying to hold one of the legs of his horse with one hand, and hammer a nail into it with the other.

It was impossible. Either the leg or his hammer kept falling. *BANG CRASH*!

The next thing she heard was someone flushing the toilet. Matt must be awake – he might come in!

"Caro!" hissed Matt from the doorway. "What are you doing? What's that noise?"

"Getting my turn on the computer," replied Carolyn gruffly. "And that's Dad, trying to put his horse together again."

Matt came over, and they looked down. "Poor old Dad," said Matt. "He'll never get it done . . ."

Then they looked at each other, both thinking the same thing: "He'll never get it done – without our help." They grinned. They were friends again.

But Carolyn hesitated. What about Helen? She must stand by her, and keep the Greeks inside the horse! But she must stand by Dad, too. He'd be shattered if his horse wasn't ready for the play.

"C'mon, Caro!" demanded Matt. "What are you waiting for?"

She decided. If Helen was magic, she could wait. Dad was human, and he couldn't.

"Let's go!" She and Matt dashed to their rooms, dragged on jeans and sweaters, and ran downstairs.

"What on earth are you two doing here?" shouted Dad. "Get back to bed!"

But when Matt grabbed a leg and held it up against the wooden horse, and Carolyn held out a hammer and a nail, he gave in.

It took them an hour and a half to finish. Carolyn and Matt worked frantically. But all the time Carolyn was thinking, "I must help Helen save Troy!"

While Dad was thanking them and hustling them back to bed, another thought came. What if the secret disk *did* help Helen save Troy? Would she *want* to stay there with Paris, who was 'not all that bright'? She might want to go back to her old home, to her husband, to Greece . . .

The streets had hardly woken up before Dad and the twins were outside.

They heaved the great horse on to the trailer, and Dad pulled the front while Carolyn and Matt pushed from behind. The milkman and the postwoman stared at them, impressed.

As they dragged the wooden horse into place in the wings of the High School stage, Carolyn's arm brushed against a long, filmy white dress on a hanger – Helen's dress!

"Thanks, you two," said Dad. "Don't know what I'd have done without you."

Matt and Carolyn grinned at each other. They knew how hard it was for Dad to say something like that.

They ran out of the gates just as the High School pupils were beginning to pour in. Carolyn had to push through a crowd of great big lads.

"Hey, junior!" said a cheerful girl's voice. "Don't get trampled underfoot!" She held up her tennis racket like a shining sword, and forced the boys to make way.

As soon as school was over, Carolyn ran home ahead of the others. She rushed upstairs and slipped the rust-brown disk into the computer. Then she blinked herself into the dream of the rust-brown horse.

Again she stood proudly, on guard beside the wooden horse. Sozzled Trojans lay snoring all around.

But – what was that creaking noise? That clash, like spears – that rattle, like armour?

Something made Carolyn look up.

The trapdoor of the wooden horse was swinging wide open. The huge cavity inside was empty.

She'd deserted her post, and while she was gone the Greeks had sneaked out. The creaking was the opening of the gates of Troy. The rattle and clash was the sound of Greek soldiers pouring through.

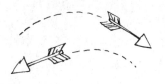

Chapter Five

Carolyn stood helpless as the battle began. The sleepy Trojans weren't fit to fight. Some of them couldn't find their swords. Everywhere Trojans were being killed by Greeks. Red blood splashed on to her hand, and tears poured down her cheeks.

She'd let Helen down! She hadn't saved Troy, hadn't helped Helen and Paris be together till the end of time!

"Helen!" she cried. "What are we going to do?" But there was no answer.

Carolyn looked all around. No sign of Helen. Then she heard a shout from behind her.

"I said I wanted to be part of the action!"

Helen was held high, carried on the shoulders of the Greeks as horde upon horde of them rushed up the beach towards Troy.

"Paris said I shouldn't fight – it would spoil my beauty! I'm not putting up with that. I'm off – I'm on the side of the Greeks now!"

At that moment, Carolyn turned round. She was just in time to see an arrow fly straight into the heart of one tall Trojan. He fell.

It was Paris. He was dead.

There was a noise on the landing. Carolyn shook herself. Was she asleep or awake? Was she inside the computer, in the High School play, or just at home, playing a computer game?

She touched her face and hands. No tears. No spattering of Trojan blood. Relief!

Matt appeared at the door. "Message from Dad," he said. "We've to go to the High right now. All hands needed on stage." And he ran back downstairs.

Carolyn was exhausted. She'd tried to change the course of history, and failed. Even Helen had deserted her, and deserted handsome Paris too. And what would she do with the rust-brown disk?

Then she started to cheer up. The Helen of her dreams was still a heroine, even if a different kind of heroine. And it'd be great helping at the High. There'd be actors, stage-hands, costume-fitters. She might even give some Greek warriors a leg-up into the belly of Dad's wooden horse.

"Caro!" came Matt's voice from below. "Hurry up!"

She rubbed her eyes, slipped the magic disk into her pocket, and ran downstairs.

The hall at the High School was bustling with people: carrying helmets, dabbing make-up on each other's faces, doing a last-minute check on lines. Carolyn heard someone say, "Have you seen that *horse*! Isn't it *wonderful*?"

She felt in her pocket for a hankie. She knew she'd cry buckets when she saw Helen on stage. Yes, the hankie was there – and so was the magic disk.

But as she took her hand out of her pocket, the disk slipped out too. She heard a *tap-tap* as it fell on to the floor.

At that moment, a voice behind her said, "It's you again. Hi!"

Carolyn whizzed round. It was the girl she'd seen carrying the tennis racket like a shining sword. Only she wasn't carrying her tennis racket now. She was wearing the long filmy white dress.

It was Helen. She wasn't in myth or in history or in dreams, and she wasn't in a computer game. She was in the play.

"Oh – hello," said Carolyn nervously. "I've just dropped a –"

"A what?"

"A kind of computer disk . . . it's down here somewhere . . ."

But it wasn't. She and Helen looked under the chair and all around. But they could find nothing. The magic disk had vanished as mysteriously as it came.

"Well," said Helen briskly. "Can you come and help me, then?"

"How?" asked Carolyn.

"Jason – the lad who's playing Paris – he thinks I'm just a pretty face," said Helen. "But I'm going to show him I'm not. I want to carry a sword in my hand."

"It's not in the story," objected Carolyn.

"I know it isn't, clever clogs," grinned Helen. "Helen's supposed to be beautiful and helpless. But that's boring."

Carolyn was horrified. "You can't change the story!" Then she realized. Changing the story was exactly what she'd wanted to do herself.

"'Course you can. Come and help me find a sword."

"Er . . ." said Carolyn, "is there time to paint it shining white?"

"Why?" asked Helen.

A voice boomed out from a loudspeaker: "All actors to the dressing room immediately! *The Trojan War* is about to begin!"

"It doesn't matter," said Carolyn. "Let's get ready for the Trojan War."

"What happened to Helen in the end?" Carolyn and Matt asked Dad.

"Oh, she went happily back to Greece. She'd loved her husband all along."

"Then why did she run off with Paris in the first place?"

"Ah," said Dad with a smile. "Venus, the goddess of love, made her do that."

"How?" they demanded.

"Off to bed," replied Dad. "That's another story."